To my big sister Elaine, with love. — B.K.

Thank you Sheina, for your help and patience... — S.B.

Phaidon Press Limited
Regent's Wharf
All Saints Street
London N1 9PA

Phaidon Press Inc.
65 Bleecker Street
New York, NY 10012

phaidon.com

First published 2018
© 2018 Phaidon Press Limited
Text copyright © Barbara Kanninen
Illustrations copyright © Serge Bloch

Artwork illustrated using collage and ink.
Typeset in Purple Regular and Futura Medium

ISBN 978 0 7148 7630 6
001-0318

A CIP catalogue record for this book is available from
the British Library and the Library of Congress.

Designed by Meagan Bennett

Printed in China

Circle rolls...

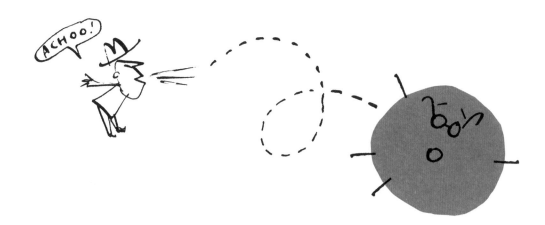

words by Barbara Kanninen art by Serge Bloch

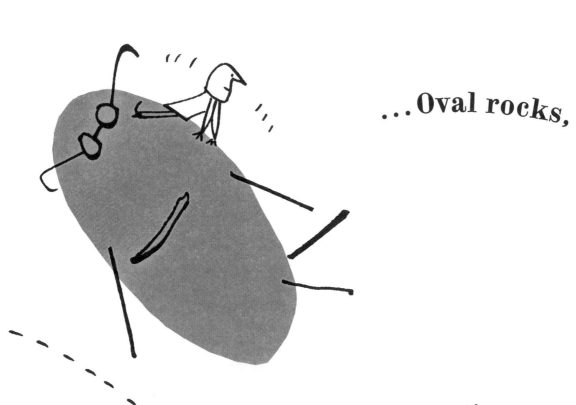

...Oval rocks,

Square sits
like a box.

Circle rolls,

Rectangle stands,

**Triangle points
without any hands.**

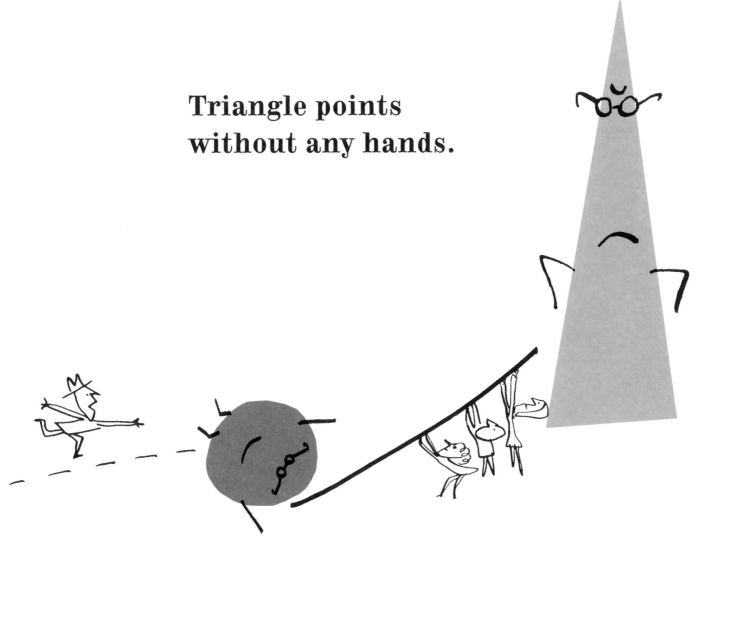

Circle rolls,

never stops,

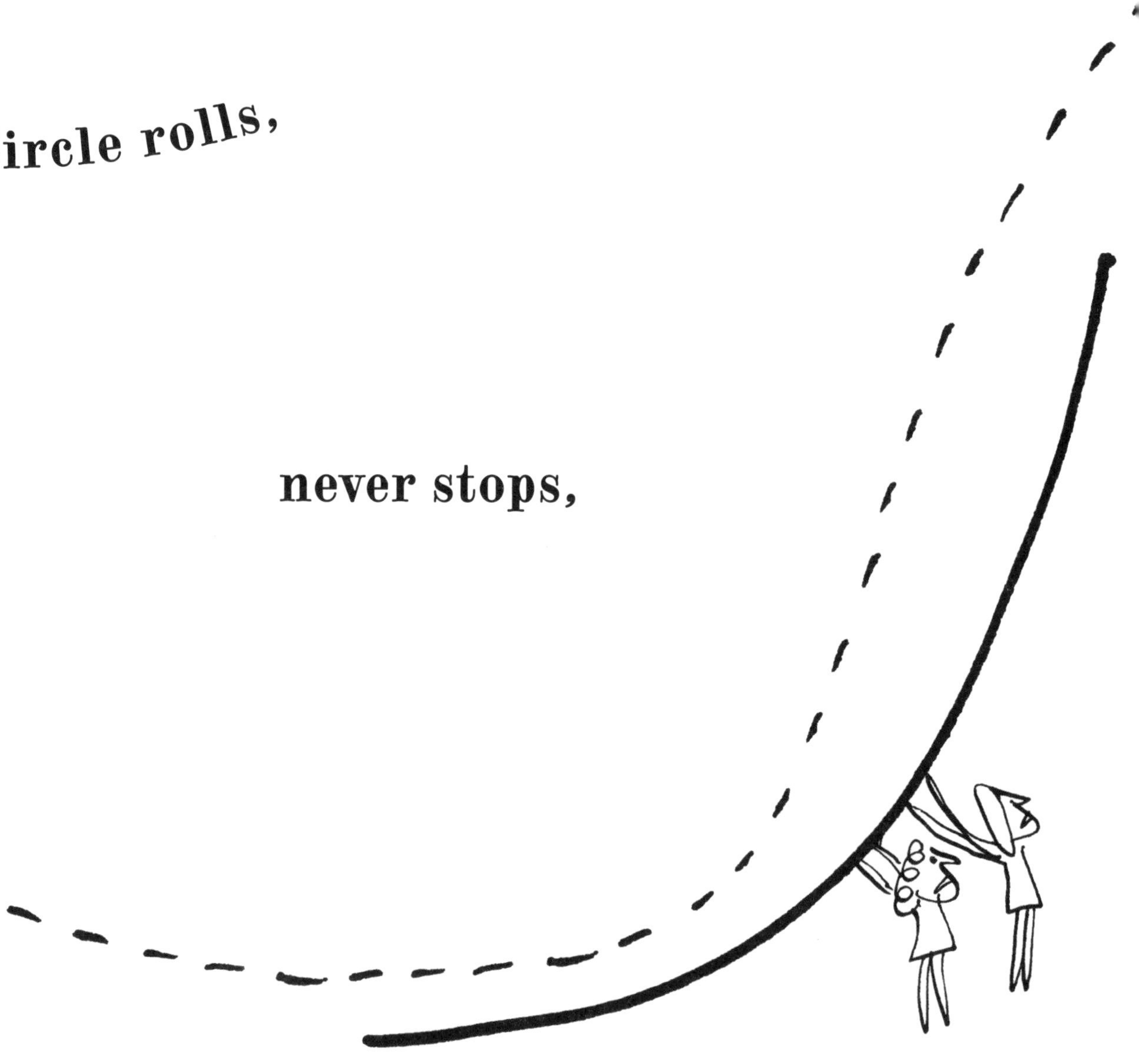

hits point . . .

CIRCLE

POPS!

**Circle drops
as tiny bits,**

**which land on Square
as it sits.**

Square sneezes,
Diamond trips,

pushes Star,
Star tips!

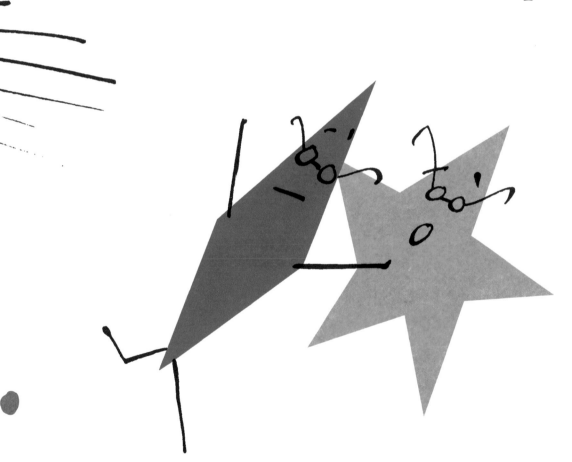

Star tumbles
end to end,

bumps Line,

makes it bend.

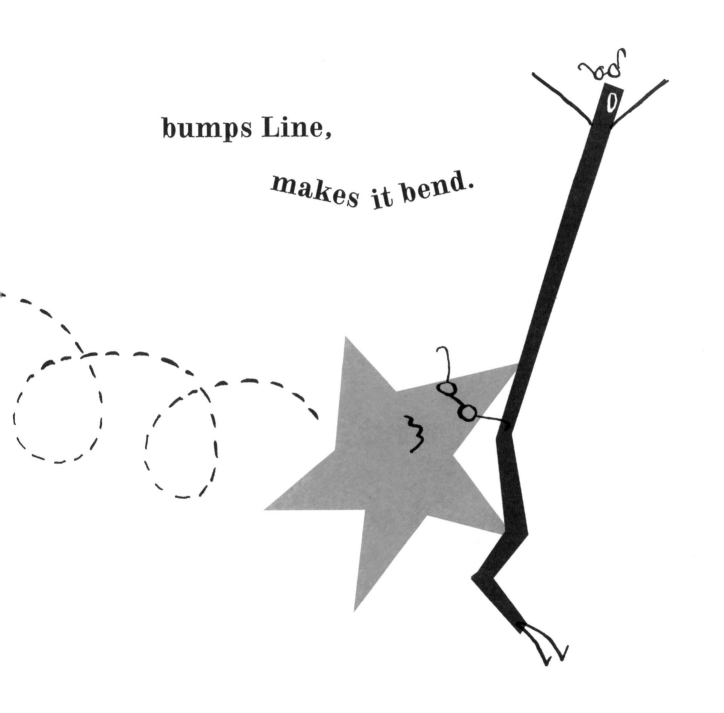

Bent Line
becomes a slide.

Shapes glide...

and fly…

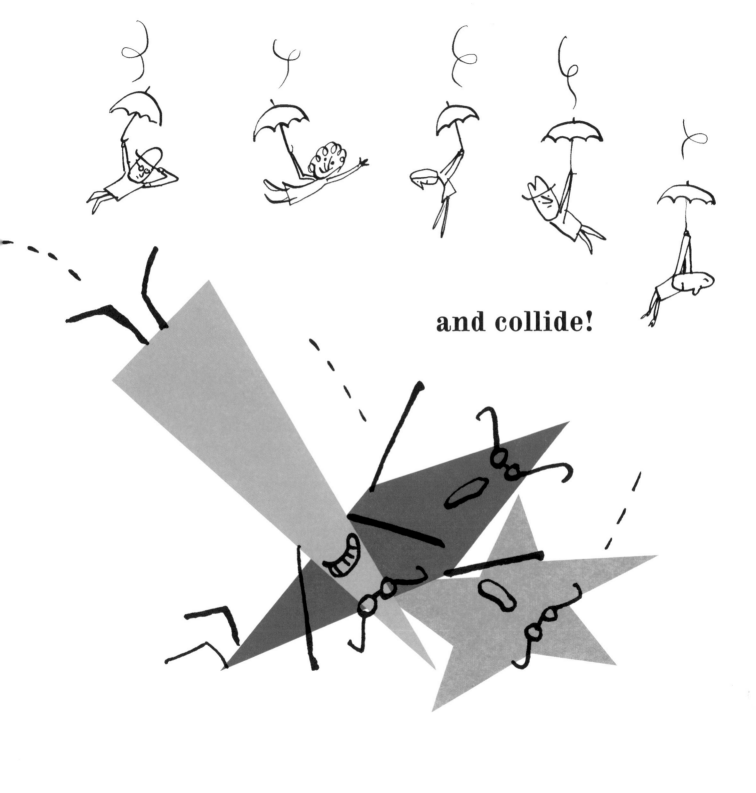

and collide!

Whirl, twirl!

Flip, flop!

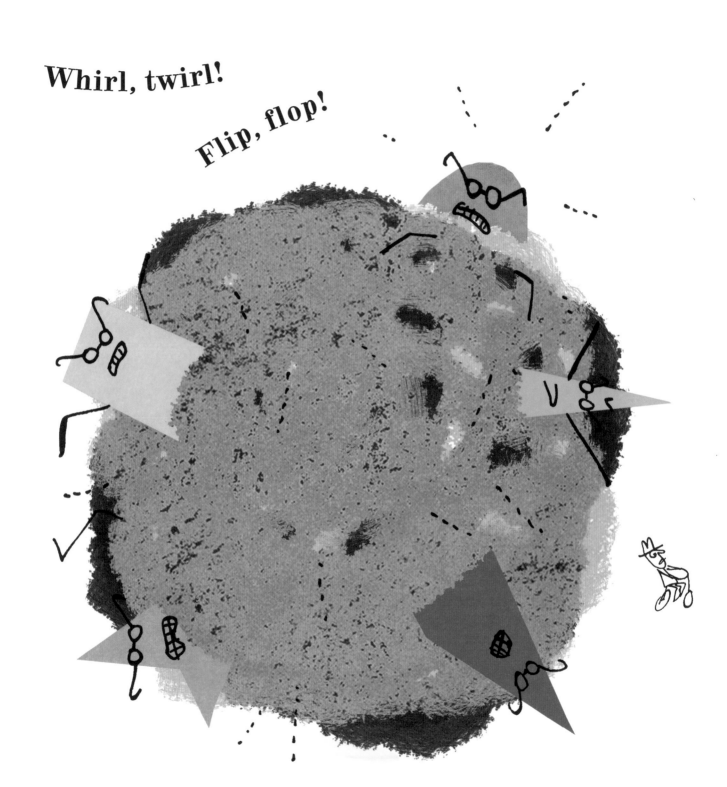

Octagon says,

"SHAPES! STOP!"

Star rises,
buffs its shine,
un-tips Diamond,

all straighten Line.

Heart appears
and gathers bits

off the ground
where Square sits.

They piece together
one bit, two,
using tape
and globs of glue.

Heart double-checks,
no more holes.

Ready, set...

Circle rolls!